I0784056

Co La La &
Co La Grr

Marija Pejakovic

Dedication

You should not want too much, but as much as is enough for happiness. You don't have to look for dreams and hopes, I'm here to make them come true for you. All this is enough to live a life full of wishes and dreams, and let this book that I am giving you always remind you of that.

Acknowledgments

Thank you mom and grandma!

About the Author

Marija Pejaković was born in 1985 in Belgrade, Serbia. Inspired by her love for children and the creative spirit she awakened during the Corona virus pandemic, she wrote a magical book for children called "Co La La & Co La Grr". This book is her imagination and dedication, which has blossomed further during the challenging times of corona. In it, you will find a rich creative experience that will enchant and entertain the little ones.

In her book "Co La La & Co La Grr", Marija carefully explores the topic of benign and malicious viruses, using stories and characters to bring children closer to the importance of health and understanding the differences between "good" and "bad" things in the world around us.

Through the pages of this book, Marija managed to convey her immense love for children and create a magical world that will inspire and make them laugh as they explore the stories from Co La La & Co La Grr.

It was a wonderful green morning. Everything should smell of flowers, buds in bloom on the trees, and breathing grass. The happy sparrows greeted themselves with their sweet singing voices. Buzzing bees were racing, which one was going to make more golden honey.

In the infinite blue sky, some clouds floated. Co la la was sitting on one of them, observing what was happening on our planet. This little ball, beetle-virus, with many small feet and hands like straws sticking out from a ball shaped body, could see exactly everything that happens in the whole world: people, cities, mountains, oceans, rivers ...sadness,joy,love ...

She happily jumped from cloud to cloud, playing and making gracious movements like a ballerina. But, she was very curious and wanted to see why the world was mantled in a gray cover.

Co la la, the little beetle virus, decided to go down to earth to discover what was actually happening.

She was flying, carrying the wind and swaying like a feather. After a long journey, she landed in a small hole on the top of an old oak., grandmothers and grandfathers were sitting underneath it, holding hands and gazing into the distance. Who could tell where their thoughts were ?!!

'Wait ... I will check,' co la la thought. Slowly, she eavesdropped to them and listened to their voices.

Grandpa: "Do you remember the shine of the grass, air that smells like green, laughter? It was all the abundance of a past world. "

Grandma:"Of course, "she said with nostalgia. She put her hand on her mouth, coughed, and continued: "I love spring because it brings a new love."

Co la la: "These old people are lovely!"

Her gaze turned to the trodden flowers in the park. People paced nervously. Some of them were arguing or sneezing.

And... Everything innocently started.

She moved on. She was flying, flying ... She stopped on the covering of the market. Apples, cabbage, spinach were lined up on the counters ... They were semi-dried, crying and singing a sad song: "Ah, ah, people, let us grow poisonless. It'll be better for us to grow in the weeds! "

Co la la was overwhelmed with sadness. She stayed for a little while, and then, in a few pirouettes, she found herself in the big hall of a building. It was written 'gymnasium' at the entrance.

"juuuu! Where am I? Which country am I in? Inshallakuwland? " the little ballerinas practiced the butterfly in the hall, in the other, they were jumping on the mats ... It was joyful, delightful everywhere in the school. Co la la was jumping, too, overwhelmed with happiness. But it lasted for a short time.

She started flying again. And she was flying, flying ... She went through the keyhole with its bally body. Then she fell to the floor. Black shadows overloaded her. The shoes were hurrying running, and she was trying to avoid sticking to their soles.

"People, what is this?" she was shouting out loud, but no one heard her.

She watched the fear, all the sadness of the world. She felt the suppressed cry of the powerless, the endless suffering of the world.

At the moment, it seemed that she saw an evil prickly ball: beetle-virus.

"yes, yes, it's him - co la grr

He came from the same place as co la la, where the two worlds collide. They shared the same air. He was menacing evil, with a big square nose. Greening, he dived into people with his spiky tentacles. He entered their nose, mouth dropping his poison.

Happy in his evil, he sluggishly sauntered. He came to ca la le. There was really something disturbing and scary at the same time in his eyes. No, co la la wasn't afraid, but she gave him a sharp eye back.

Co la grr was flying around co la la and murmured in a rude voice: "Ha, ha, ha ... You can't do anything to me! My saw tentacles are reaching everywhere and into everyone. You deserve it! Darkness is my weapon. Nothing will save you!" And in one instance, he enters the nose of a grandpa. Then he ran out, thrown out like a catapult, and said, "yea, I will not let them breathe! I`ll spray them with my poison, I'll enter into the one, the other, the hundreds ... I`ll have a crazy fun, ahahaha! "

He conquered the whole world. Everything stopped. Cities were spooky. Silence was everywhere. Most people were trying to forget everything that happened during the day and believed that everything was just an ugly dream.

Co la la: "My time has come, my free flight for the salvation of the innocent! I will make a storm of my exhalation, and the world will breathe the new life! "

She turned on all her powers. Her numerous legs and hands emitted powerful energy and yellow light that looked like fire. She swore that no one would cry the river tears in which the pain for those who loved was stored.

"I`m coming, co la grr! I will break you like a stick! "

Along with the music of the spring waltz, a waltz of love, she started with big jumps.

She was flying, crossing the mountains, deserts ...the sea currents threw her everywhere, sometimes she had to rest on the mast of some ship. The will for a world to be clean did not leave her. She followed the smell of co la grra. He was trying to cheat co la lu. The fragrances of the sky, ocean, and vanilla filled her tubes ...

"yeah, I feel he is close!"

She slowed down and braked with her propellers.

She saw co la grra on a giant flower magically colored. He dissolved his round body. His arms and legs fell on the petals. He looked like a filled ball that would explode any time.

"Oh, there you are, carrying a fuzzy villain!"

"aaaaaaa!" he yawned, appearing not interested: "what do you want?"

"I want you to immediately stop entering the noses and mouths of innocent people and discharge your poison!"

"hahahaha! You are really funny and stupid thick ball that acts good. There is nothing more fun! I close their noses; they can't breathe! They are slowly leaving this world that is becoming mine! I will be the ruler of the air on the whole planet! ”

He continued to jabber, jabber, jabber ...

“Think quickly, co la la!” she repeated to herself.

Finally she figured it out! ”co la grr, can you move a little bit so that I can lie next to you on that giant flower?” she said.

" mmmmmmm, you`ll join me - that is good!" he replied. He had no idea what she was going to do.

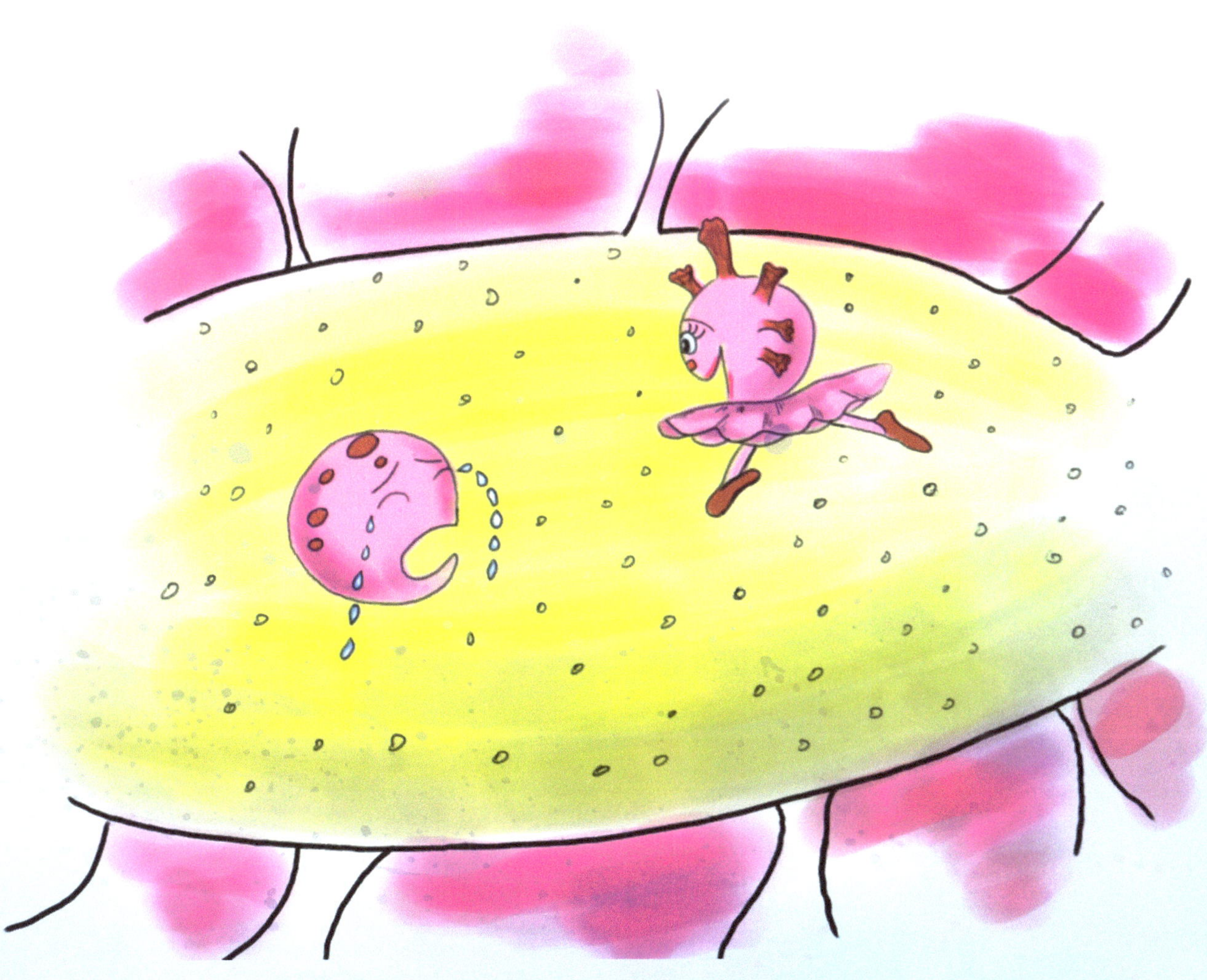

She lay down next to him. She stretched out one of her legs and pricked a blue petal that was right under his leg. Blue petal juice touched his leg and - look at that miracle! The foot dried off!

"ouch! What's going on? What`s burning me? I can't move my leg! "co la grr moaned.

"now you`ll see!" she did the same thing with pink, red, green, purple petal.

He couldn`t move. His ball body was all that remained.

"What did you do to me, you...!" he became enraged while he was squirming.

"Just a little more, there is only a body under the yellow pestle of the magical flower. Uhh! What will I do if I fail?! I must succeed! I have to! " co la la repeated to herself.

She stretched her arms and legs, intertwined them in a ponytail, and twisted her ball-shaped body to reach the middle of the magical flower.

"I can`t! Uhhh! My legs are too short! "

come on, co la la, use your nose quickly!

She removed the ballet shoes, which difficult to access. With its top, she was able to reach the yellow middle of the flower.

Co la grr started to screw up in pain. His body changed colors like a traffic light, and at the same time, it was wasting away. He tried to say something, but the yellow flower juice burned him at an unseen speed. All that left was a stain on a giant flower.

Co la la moved her tired body. She released from the flower and watched in co la grra. It looked like a smashed, burned pea.

She was overjoyed. She believed that the guide to salvation was in the nature. She activated her propellers and moved.

The gray cover above the world disappeared. The green world filled with love and happiness was raised again. Everyone inhaled that new world. Along with the music of the spring waltz, co la la was sitting on a cloud, dancing, guarding the world from another beetle virus.